Zed Storm has lived in Japan for the past five years and is a master of several martial arts.

He has a wolfhound called Max, and in his spare time plays the guitar and competes in triathlons. He likes to read about history, space exploration and rare animals and he came up with the idea for Will Solvit whilst camping in a Siberian Forest.

ATTENTION: ALL READERS!

Wherever you see something that looks like this, reach for your decoder! Holding it by the corner, place the centre of your decoder over the lines. Rotate it very slowly, look closely and a picture will appear.

Mystery solved!

AND THE T-REX TERROR

PaRRagon

Bath · New York · Singapore · Hong Kong · Cologne · Delhi · Melbourne

Written by Zed Storm
Creative concept and words by E. Hawken
Check out the website at **www.will-solvit.com**

First edition published by Parragon in 2010

Parragon
Queen Street House
4 Queen Street
Bath BA1 1HE, UK

ISBN 978-1-4075-8982-4

Printed in UK

Please retain this information for future reference.

CONTENTS

rrraaaarrr

yuk

?

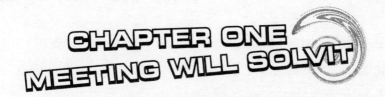

It's not always easy being ten years old. I might get to take my skateboard out on Saturdays, blast aliens to dust on my games console and read comic books, but sometimes life can be tough. My dad's an inventor, you see. It might sound cool, but sometimes it can make life pretty difficult. Some of the stuff Dad invents is really impressive – like the lunar-powered X-ray binoculars that almost won him a Nobel Prize. But for every great invention there are a thousand not-so-great ones – take the fart-powered jet skis that he came up with last Christmas!

And it's not just Dad's inventions that make

life difficult – I'm always getting into trouble at school, too. It's not like I go looking for problems, they just have a way of finding me. Today I accidentally set a battery-charged dinosaur at my teacher's feet and she skidded on it and went flying out of the classroom. I got detention for that one...

Actually, detention wasn't so bad, cuz I was able to read a book. Reading can be pretty fun – all that stuff about aliens, monsters and dinosaurs.

I love dinosaurs – along with computer games and comic books, they're pretty much my favourite things. I've learned tons about dinosaurs from books. Check out my top three dinosaur facts:

- **Some species of dinosaurs were as big as a bus and others were as small as a chicken!**
- **No one knows exactly what colour dinosaurs**

were – I like to imagine that they were blue and green, my favourite colours.
- Instead of chewing their food, some dinosaurs swallowed stones that would grind up food in their stomachs.

I'm telling you all this because of something strange that happened to me in detention that afternoon – I was halfway through this really awesome chapter about the Velociraptors when I turned the page and saw an envelope with my name on it. I didn't recognize the handwriting (it was definitely a grown-up's, though), but it really was addressed to me – Will Solvit.

I looked up to check that my teacher wasn't watching – she wasn't – and ripped open the top of the envelope. Inside was a small piece of paper. This is what it said:

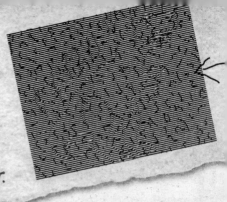

I turned the envelope upside down to check that there was nothing else in it, but there wasn't. How weird is that? Who had put the envelope there and what did it mean?

Anyway, before I knew it, detention was over and Dad had arrived to pick me up in Sputnik. Luckily none of the other kids were around to see our super-weird car. Dad built it. It runs on vegetable oil and makes a noise like an exploding rhino bum when it fires off down the road.

Luckily, Dad was too busy telling me about a mile-high pogo stick that he'd been working on to worry about the fact that I'd been in detention,

~ Bit whiffy!

and obviously I didn't tell him about the weird letter I'd found. Whoever had written it had told me to keep it a secret.

"So, Will," Dad said after a while, "what was the best thing about school today?"

"I read a book about dinosaurs," I answered. "Did you know that the Stegosaurus had spikes all over its back so that the other dinosaurs couldn't attack it – how cool is that?"

"Aha! But did you know that the Stegosaurus was the size of a bus? Or that its favourite food was bananas?" Dad answered.

You see, Dad always knows more about stuff than me. He's better than me at pretty much everything. Except for computer games – I always beat him at those.

"Really? Weird," I said. "I hate bananas – squishy, yucky monkey food. You know, it would be so cool to actually see a dinosaur."

"Well, funny you should say that," said Dad. "I thought we might do just that this weekend."

"Not a museum again," I groaned. As far as I was concerned, Museums = Boredom.

"No, Will," Dad laughed, "not a museum. I'm going to take you to see a living, breathing dinosaur. A real live one. We're going back in time!"

"Back in time! With the Morphometer! That's awesome!" I breathed, my eyes nearly popping out of my head in shock.

You see, that's another thing I should have told you about

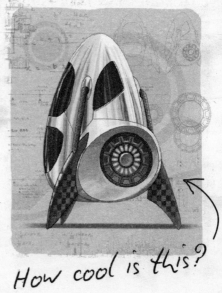

How cool is this?

my dad. He doesn't just invent everyday things. He invents pretty extraordinary things too. Like the Morphometer (or Morph for short) – a machine that can morph into anything you want it to be – submarine, helicopter, racing car, parachute, even a time machine! It makes the best sound when it transforms – kind of like a light saber. The coolest thing about it is that once you've finished using it, it shrinks down so small you can fit it in your pocket, and it always looks like the last thing you used it for, which is kind of fun. Once it looked like a miniature bumper car for a whole week!

Dad laughed. "Yes, this Saturday... I thought we could see just how far back in time Morph can actually take us."

"Awesome!" I shouted as Sputnik made an extra-loud fart noise.

"Well, that's settled, then," Dad beamed.

"Saturday it is. I'll have to check with Mum, of course."

Sputnik seemed to agree. As we turned the corner to home, he made an extra-wet, extra-loud, spluttery noise...

Spluuuuuurrrrrrrrpppp!

"WILL SOLVIT!" a voice called out as I pushed back the front door.

Although Dad hadn't asked me too much about detention, Mum was obviously not going to let me off the hook that easily. "So," she said, "tell me exactly what happened."

"Well, Mum, uh... it went something like this..."

And so I told her everything – from putting the

dinosaur on the floor to the part about Mrs Davies skidding out of the room on the back of it. I could see that Mum was trying to keep a straight face. That's the thing about Mum, you see. She might seem all strict, but underneath it all she likes to have a laugh, too.

Mum's name is Edith (Dad is Henry) but her friends call her Eddy. I just call her Mum. She used to have a job in a cake-baking factory before I was born, putting cherries on top of cupcakes. That's how she met my dad – he didn't work in the bakery, though, he's always been an inventor. One day he flew through the factory window and flattened all her cakes!

Dad was taking his new glider for a spin when, just as he was soaring over my mum's bakery, he had to make an emergency crash landing and smashed right through a window next to where

Mum sat. Apparently he had cherries stuck all over his bottom when they pulled him off the mangled cakes. But as soon as Mum lifted the broken glider wing from his face, it was love at first sight!

I wish that Mum still worked in that bakery – imagine all the free cakes we'd get!

Anyway, that's probably enough about Mum – especially since she was giving me a look that said if I didn't get up the stairs and do my homework right now I'd be put to work setting the table instead. And so, without a backwards glance, I shot out through the door and up the stairs to my room...

Saturday couldn't come quickly enough for me.
But eventually there were just three more days
of school, then two, then one… and finally it was
the weekend and there we all were, sitting in the
steel-plated laboratory that was added on to the
side of our house, waiting to try out Morph.

"OK, so let me just find the right program,"
said Dad as he looked through his memory chips.
He took one out and inserted it into the side of
Morph. He pressed his thumb on an X-ray pad,
and Morph morphed into a large, freestanding
time machine. Mum, Dad and I stepped inside.

"Now, Will, it's very important that you don't
touch anything – the flick of a wrong switch and

17

we could end up completely lost in time and space," said Dad, tapping some words into a computer screen and pushing a large button...

Sparks flew and green squiggles flashed across the screen, and before I knew it, Morph was whizzing back in time...

Stepping out of a time machine and into a prehistoric jungle is fantastic. It's like having your birthday, Christmas and the last day of school all at once. Everywhere I looked there were tropical flowers, and ancient flies buzzed around my head (my arms soon got tired from swatting them away).

"So, how far back in time do you think we've travelled, Dad?" I asked, as my feet crunched down on the jungle ground.

"I'd say about five million years before the dinosaurs became extinct, which was sixty-five million years ago," he replied.

I did the maths in my head. "So we've travelled back seventy million years!"

"That's correct, Will." Dad led the way through the forest and held branches back so that Mum and I could follow behind him. He pointed at trees and got excited about the bugs crawling all over them. Taking out his magnifying glass, he held it up to a nearby leaf.

"Come here, Will," he said. "You see this insect..."

I looked at the bug. It had about a hundred legs and its body was a mixture of green and red splotches.

"This is a very special insect," Dad said. "It

likes to sink its fangs into dinosaurs and drink their blood."

"Cool!" I replied.

Mum made a disgusted face. I don't think she likes bugs very much – especially not the type that suck blood!

We were getting deeper and deeper into the jungle and still I hadn't seen a dinosaur.

"Daaaaaaad?" I asked. "Why haven't we seen any dinosaurs yet?"

"Be patient, Will," said Dad. "Dinosaurs can be very shy, you know!"

Suddenly I could hear a loud cawwww coming from the skies. It didn't sound like any bird I'd heard before. I looked up and, sure enough, a winged dinosaur was flying around above us. I was too shocked to speak.

"That's a Raptor," Dad informed me.

The real-life Raptor was bigger than pictures in books. It was probably the coolest thing I'd ever seen in my entire life. Mum looked at the sky nervously and then kept going.

Dad had to drag me forwards – I didn't want to keep walking. I wanted to stay right where I was so that I could look at the Raptor some more.

We walked for ages. It was really hot in the jungle, and I was getting very sweaty. Dad kept trying to tell me about the different trees that we were walking past:

"Did you know that you can tell a tree's age by counting the number of rings in its trunk?" he said. "And the oldest tree fossil known to man is three hundred eighty-five million years old. Fossilized trees are often called 'petrified trees'."

"Can we see another dinosaur?" I asked.

"There are trees and leaves and creepy-crawlies

back home."

"Let's sit here," Mum said, ignoring me. I had been so busy thinking about dinosaurs that I'd forgotten about the lunch we'd brought with us. Suddenly the thought of food made me really hungry.

Mum threw down a picnic blanket. She started unpacking a basket of sandwiches. There was also a salad in a large tub. I quickly picked up a plastic plate and started loading it high with peanut-butter-and-jam sandwiches, pretending I hadn't seen the salad. I took a huge bite and started to chew. That's when I heard it...

A rustling noise coming from somewhere in the jungle. My jaw froze in mid-chew.

It was getting louder.

And louder.

And LOUDER!

Dad stood up and slowly walked towards the rustling sound. "Well…" he whispered.

I gulped down the contents of my mouth and got to my feet.

"Is it a dinosaur, Dad?" I asked.

"I'm not too sure…" was all he said.

Crunch. Snap. Shuffle.

I could hear it getting closer.

First came two twitching nostrils. Then a crinkled snout appeared from between the jungle bushes. Then two birdlike eyes peered out at me.

Slowly, it walked towards us. It wasn't very

tall – about my height. Its stumpy body looked like a bald, overgrown chicken, and it was the colour of mud, which was a bit disappointing (I'd really hoped dinosaurs would be blue and green).

"Aha!" My dad pointed one finger in the air and his face split into a wide grin. "A Bugenasaura!"

"A Bugen – what?" I asked.

"A Bugenasaura," Dad repeated. "A very rare species from the Upper Cretaceous period."

The Bugenasaura made a strange quacking sound and took a step towards me. I flinched backwards.

"Oh, no need to be worried, Will," Dad reassured me. "It's perfectly safe. The Bugenasaura is a vegetarian – he won't want to eat us."

Mum shrieked as the Bugenasaura waddled towards her salad. She tried to pull the bowl out of the way, but she wasn't fast enough. The small dinosaur bent down and took a large mouthful. He munched merrily, spitting tomato seeds everywhere!

Now the Bugenasaura was shuffling off towards the thicket again and Mum and Dad kept eating and talking about trees – but I had other ideas. I sneaked away from my parents and followed the Bugenasaura. I wanted to see if he'd lead me to any other dinosaurs. It would be fantastic to see some more before I went home.

The dinosaur walked around in circles for ages – Bugenasauras obviously aren't very smart! But after a while his nose started to twitch and he walked deeper into the jungle.

"Be careful, Will," Dad shouted as I followed the dinosaur. "Don't go too far."

"I won't," I said.

I didn't need to go far. The Bugenasaura started to chew on the leaves of a yellow bush. Underneath the bush was something really cool – a dinosaur nest!

The nest was huge, and dug into a mound of earth that sat about three feet above the ground. The inside of the nest was full of leaves and twigs, and in the middle were six large dinosaur eggs.

A thought flashed into my mind – at the time it seemed like the best idea I'd ever had. I could take an egg. I could take the egg back home and hatch it and have my very own dinosaur! A Bugenasaura would make the perfect pet dinosaur: not too small, not too big, and it was a herbivore so there was no danger of it growing up and eating me!

I crept into the nest and slipped one of the

large eggs into my bag. It was surprisingly heavy. The Bugenasaura didn't seem to mind what I was doing, although I did feel a tiny bit of doubt about taking the egg from her nest. What if she missed it?

"I promise I'll take good care of it after it hatches," I whispered, as she continued to munch on leaves.

I tried not to look suspicious as I walked back into the clearing towards Mum and Dad. There was no way they'd let me take a dinosaur egg back home. I would just have to keep quiet about it until we were back – that way it would be too late to do anything about it.

"Dad?" I asked.

"Yes, Will?"

"Do you think the Bugenasaura is the only dinosaur we'll get close to today?"

"Well, Will…" Dad began. Suddenly he was cut off by a large thud echoing through the jungle. The ground vibrated underneath my feet and the leaves on the trees above my head shook.

Thud. Thud.

It sounded like the footsteps of something larger than an elephant and heavier than a house!

Thud. Thud.

I looked over at Dad – he had turned whiter than a ghost.

Thud. Thud.

The Bugenasaura froze. He started making weird squealy noises and running around in a circle. He seemed to know what was heading our way…

THUD. THUD.

The noise was getting louder now. It was then that I realized my wish was about to come true. I was going to see a REAL dinosaur – one that was big and scary and had footsteps heavy enough to make the ground shake. I was going to meet a dinosaur that wanted to eat more than just salad! I was about to meet a Tyrannosaurus rex!

TOTALLY AWESOME!

From the trip to the prehistoric jungle

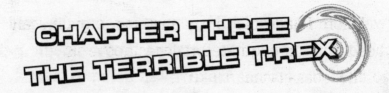

CHAPTER THREE
THE TERRIBLE T-REX

"Rooooaaaaaaaaarrrrrrrrr!!!!!!!!"

My hands clapped against the sides of my head as my ears rang with pain.

"Rooooaaaaaaaaarrrrrrrrr!!!!!!!!"

"Dad!" I cried in terror.

"Whatever you do," Dad said calmly, "keep very, very still."

I gulped. Something about the sound of that roar told me that keeping still could be a bad idea.

Dad could see the look on my face. "Don't worry," he said. "He won't see us unless we move."

"But Dad…"

Before I had time to say anything, a giant scaly head burst through the branches above us.

"Rooooaaaaaaaaaarrrrrrrrrr!!!!!!!!"

The huge T-rex was only a few yards away. He was massive; my head didn't even come up to his kneecap! He stood on his two back legs and held his tiny arms into his puffed-out chest. The Tyrannosaurus rex was my favourite dinosaur. I liked the T-rex more than any other dinosaur for these reasons:

- It was the fiercest dinosaur known – every other dinosaur was scared of it.
- It had teeth the size of bananas – fact!
- It could smell you from miles away – even if you were really clean.
- It was the largest predator to live on land – EVER!

The dinosaur stomped towards us. We did as Dad said and kept as still as statues. I'd read enough about T-rexes to know that they are incredibly dangerous and that a human-shaped snack would be just his thing.

"Rooooaaaaaaaaaarrrrrrrrrr!!!!!!!!"

He was so close now, his roar was louder than thunder and made the skin on my face ripple like a wave. I could even feel the egg inside my backpack shake from the vibration.

His head bent down and his tiny eyelids blinked curiously. Dad was right, the T-rex didn't seem to see us. He could smell us, though – I could tell by the way his nostrils were twitching.

In the middle of his giant face sat the sharpest set of teeth I had ever seen – each tooth like a giant steak knife inside his mouth. No book I had read had ever described just how sharp a T-rex's teeth were, or just how bad his breath smelled. It smelled like old farts.

Suddenly there was a shrill shrieking noise coming from beside me – the Bugenasaura. I'd completely forgotten that she was so close. Up until then the small dinosaur had been as still and quiet as us. But now she was making a pathetic crying noise!

The T-rex stood tall and roared again. "Rooooaaaaaaaaaarrrrrrrrrr!"

His tiny arms twitched next to his body, and his sharp claws curled with excitement. I knew what was coming.

The Bugenasaura waddled into the clearing and started to run around in circles again – as if that was going to save her.

What happened next was so quick, so disgusting, so violent, and so cool, I still wonder if

I did actually see it...

The T-rex's huge head bent down towards the squealing Bugenasaura. Giant jaws snapped around the little dinosaur, and the Bugenasaura's small body popped like a balloon. Red dinosaur blood splattered around us. Her tiny legs jerked around as the T-rex sucked them into his mouth.

When the T-rex had finished, he slowly swiped his pink tongue over his scaly lips. Tilting his head to one side, he peered at us and blinked.

"Don't worry." Dad's voice shook as he spoke. "He can only see us if we move."

"But can he hear us?" I asked.

"Rooooaaaaaaaaaarrrrrrrrrr!" boomed the T-rex.

"Run, Will!" Dad screamed in panic.

Without thinking, I bolted as fast as I could.

I could hear the T-rex running behind me.

I could hear the thump of his footsteps shake the

forest and his hot stinky breath tickle the back of my neck.

I can run pretty fast – I play football, baseball and tennis – but I was no match for a T-rex. I ran in zigzags, hoping to confuse him, but it didn't seem to slow him down.

"Dad!" I shouted as I ran. "Dad, Mum! Where are you?"

"Keep running, Will!" Mum's voice was far away, but I could tell she was shouting.

"We'll run a different way and try to distract the T-rex," Dad called through the jungle. "You run back to Morph and wait for us inside. As soon as we've lost this terrible T-rex we'll be right behind you."

I did as I was told. I ran and ran through the jungle. Maybe Dad would shoot the T-rex with a tranquilizing dart? Or maybe he'd use a language

voice chip to speak to him in T-rex – that way
Dad could ask him to leave us alone. Better
still, he could whistle to attract another dinosaur
towards us – then the T-rex could eat him instead.

But the T-rex wasn't following Mum and Dad
– he was following me. He was right on my tail
– stomping and roaring from behind as if he was
really angry. As I peered over my shoulder, I saw
cold eyes staring straight back at me.

I made a sharp left turn. The sound of the T-rex
footsteps wasn't as loud – I was losing him. Mum
and Dad must have managed to distract him after
all. I kept on running as fast as I could, just
in case.

Before I knew it I'd run all of the way back
to Morph. I opened the door and dashed inside.
Taking my backpack off, I carefully put it down on
the floor. For a moment I couldn't think why the

bag was so heavy, and then I remembered… the egg.

I figured that Dad and Mum would want to get out of the jungle as soon as possible. So to get ready, I tapped "home" in the keys on Morph's keyboard, like Dad had done before. Now I just needed my parents.

It was quiet for a moment. I managed to catch my breath. Running through a hot, sticky jungle had made me very tired.

I had just started to calm down when I heard the footsteps again.

THUD. THUD.

They were pretty loud and getting louder, which meant that they were really close. Mum and Dad must be running towards me, with the T-rex close behind.

"Rooooaaaaaaaaarrrrrrrrr!" boomed the T-Rex.

I didn't know what to do, but I had to do something. Quickly, I pressed my thumb onto the X-ray pad like I'd seen Dad do before.

The sounds around me were soon replaced by the whizzing and gushing of travelling through millions of years.

It had worked – Morph had left the jungle and was heading back to the future.

But, as Morph landed on my dad's laboratory floor with a loud clunk, I realized three things...

I was home. I was safe. But Mum and Dad had been left behind with man-eating dinosaurs, without a time machine to bring them back!

CHAPTER FOUR
HOME ALONE!

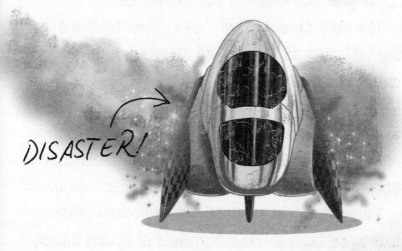

DISASTER!

I squeezed my eyes tight, hoping that I was
dreaming. Everything had happened so quickly
that it didn't seem real. Smoke was coming out of
Morph's engine and sparks were flying out of the
control panel.

I lay on the floor of the time machine, the backpack with the stolen dinosaur egg by my feet.

I had to fix Morph. I had to get back in time to rescue Mum and Dad. But I didn't have a clue how. Why had I never paid attention in science class? Listening to the whirr of the dying engine, I stared at the papers fluttering around me. Sketches of Morph's engine, sheets of equations – none of it meant anything to me without Dad there to explain it.

Then I noticed an envelope, addressed to me. It was peeping out between bits of falling paper, and looked exactly like the one I'd found in the dinosaur book at school.

I didn't have time to read it now. I stuffed the envelope into my pocket and got to my feet. Morph's engine started making a strange spluttering noise, like it was sneezing.

Suddenly, the awful sounds got louder... and louder. The lights inside the time machine began to flash like a disco. The door flew open and I felt a gust of invisible force pull me up and send me flying. I flew through the air, out of the time machine and onto the laboratory floor.

Bump!

I crashed down, bum first, onto the steel floor of Dad's laboratory. My backpack landed next to me with a thud. I turned around to see Morph's door slam shut and heard the clunking of mechanical locks bolting – Morph was locking me out! There was the sound of a dying engine – like a broken whistle. Then Morph's lights went out.

I ran up and banged my hands against the time machine door, hoping it would open again. It was my only way to rescue Mum and Dad!

I beat my clenched fists against the metal door

until they hurt. I was in mid-thump when Morph shrank from a full-size time machine back to a tiny model that I could fit in the palm of my hand.

Morph's side popped open. The memory chip that had turned Morph into a fully operational time machine was crushed. I'd never be able to fix that.

I picked up the pocket-sized Morph and began shaking and poking it, desperately trying to bring it to life again.

I was so busy poking Morph that it took me a while to see my backpack shaking.

The backpack toppled over, and out rolled the dinosaur egg that I had stolen.

It had cracked. But whatever was inside of it was still very much alive. A tiny, scaly claw was poking through the eggshell. The claw wiggled, making the hole bigger. Soon there was enough room for a small, birdlike eye to peer through.

The egg split in half. A gooey, scaly baby stretched its legs and made a gunky gurgle.

Its tiny head tilted to one side, and its eyes blinked at me.

It wasn't a baby Bugenasaura at all. I knew right away what was staring back at me, and suddenly I knew why the T-rex had chased me through the jungle. He hadn't been a he at all. He had been a she! No wonder she had been so mad at me. It was just that I had something that belonged to her – an egg.

A giant T-rex egg!

OMG!!!

This is → NOT a Bugenasaura!

"Oh, no," I whispered, holding my breath. I didn't want to do anything to catch the baby T-rex's attention.

Slowly, I took a side step towards the laboratory door. The tiny T-rex took a clumsy step towards me.

I froze. I didn't want to make any sudden movements. I was on my own and no one was going to help me escape a T-rex for the second time that day.

It purred.

I stayed deadly still as it took a few more shaky steps in my direction, and it purred again, as if it was asking for something.

The baby dinosaur tilted its head to the side once more, and the terrible truth dawned on me: the baby T-rex thought I was its mum!

All my life I'd wanted a pet T-rex – Mum

always used to tell me to be careful what I wished for cuz it might come true. She was right!

He was small but dangerous. I didn't have to get close to realize that. With those teeth he could do some serious damage. But despite the teeth, I felt sorry for him and bad about what I'd done. He belonged in a jungle, not an inventor's laboratory. I'd brought him here, so he would have to be my responsibility. Looking into his little eyes, I knew that it would have to be my job to make sure that he got home safely, and until he did, I'd have to look after him.

"It's OK, Rex." (I'd always wanted to call a pet T-rex "Rex.") "I'll take care of you." But soon enough...

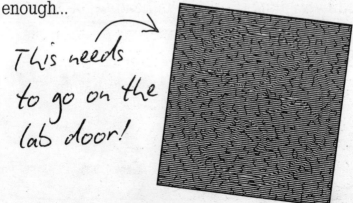

This needs to go on the lab door!

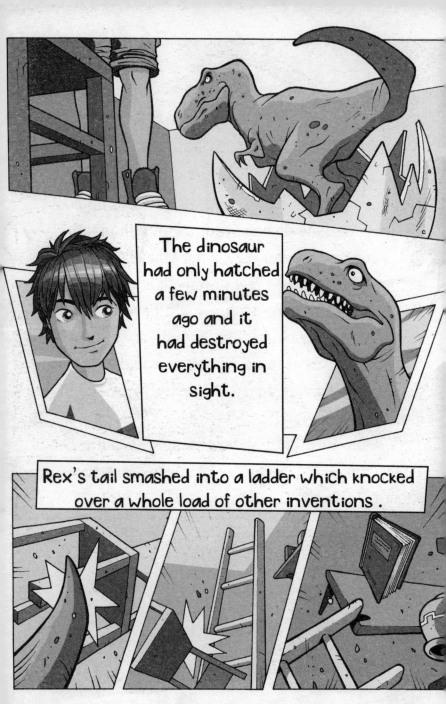

The dinosaur had only hatched a few minutes ago and it had destroyed everything in sight.

Rex's tail smashed into a ladder which knocked over a whole load of other inventions.

I knew I had to act fast. If I didn't, he would eat my leg in no time at all!

Then I saw it. A spray can had landed at my feet when the shelves fell down. My dad's deadly fart gas. It seemed a little mean, but it was my only hope.

It could have gone totally wrong, but it was a risk I had to take. Blasting my new pet with noxious fart spray was my only chance of escape. I flicked my toe at the bottom of the can as if it was a football. It flew through the air towards me and into my hands. Pressing the nozzle down, I unleashed the deadly fart gas into Rex's mouth.

He started to gag. His watery eyes looked up at me in shock and horror. Before I had time to feel guilty, his eyelids fluttered shut and his little body went limp and fell to the ground.

Quickly I stepped away from him. His small,

scaly chest was gently rising and falling – he was still breathing.

"Phew!" I thought.

I breathed a sigh of relief and stepped towards the laboratory door. I turned the door handle and slipped into the main house. Closing the door behind me, I locked it shut and tried not to worry about the mess behind it. I had to think about what to do next...

One thing they don't teach you at school is what to do when you've travelled back millions of years in time, accidentally left your parents there and brought back a dinosaur egg that hatched into a T-rex who thinks you're its mum.

Figuring things out was going to be tough. I walked through my empty house, wondering how I should deal with the sticky situation I'd got myself into.

And so I picked up the phone and called the only person I knew could help, the only person I could tell the truth to – Grandpa Monty...

Grandpa Monty Solvit is my dad's dad. He lives in a big, old house called Solvit Hall in the middle of the countryside and talks to himself a lot.

Grandpa has a dog called Plato. Not any old dog – a Westie, which means he looks like the head of a mop. His fur is seriously fluffy and bright white. Someone told me once that dogs and their owners look alike, and this is definitely true of Grandpa and Plato.

Anyway, I called Grandpa up. It went something like this:

"Hi Grandpa, it's Will."

"Will?"

"Yes, Grandpa. Will... your grandson."

"Grandson?"

"Yes... William... remember?"

"William? How are you, my boy? Good to hear from you!"

"Grandpa, something bad has happened and I need your help..."

And so I told Grandpa everything... about going back in time... about coming back by myself... about Mum and Dad being left behind... and that I'd accidentally brought back a baby T-rex with me. Then he spoke...

"How do you know about Morph? Such powerful inventions are not the business of young boys."

After my whole story, that was all he had to say?

I think Grandpa was missing the point here. What was the big deal about knowing about Morph when I'd just told him I'd left Mum and Dad behind in the middle of Jurassic Park!

"It's going to be OK," Grandpa said. "Stay where you are and I'll send a car for you. You can come and stay with me."

"But what about Mum and Dad?" I said.

"Don't you worry, I'm sure they'll be fine. They'll probably be back by dinnertime. Go and pack your bag."

"But Grandpa..." I started.

It was too late. Grandpa had hung up the phone, and the line had gone dead...

Grandpa's phone isn't mobile!

CHAPTER FIVE
SOLVIT HALL

So I did as Grandpa Monty told me and went upstairs to my room to pack.

I picked up a stack of my favourite comic books, my games, my baseball and my MP3 player before stashing them in the biggest bag I could find. I didn't bring any of my dinosaur books with me – I'd had enough dinosaurs to last me a lifetime. I didn't bother bringing any clothes either, other than what I was wearing. After all, you can wear underpants for at least a week, then you can turn them inside out and wear them for another!

I slung my bag over my shoulder and rested my hand on the edge of my trouser pocket. My fingers brushed against paper. The envelope that I'd found inside Morph – it was still there!

I dropped my heavy bag, pulled the envelope out and quickly ripped it open. My eyes studied the page, taking in every word...

HOW DOES A DINOSAUR FEEL WHEN IT HURTS ITS TOE?

DINO-SORE!

MONTY HAS A SECRET.
ALL IS NOT AS IT SEEMS.
DON'T LEAVE THE HOUSE UNTIL YOU'VE PACKED EVERYTHING YOU NEED.
TAKE TOOLS FOR AN ADVENTURE.

Secret? Tools? Adventure?

Who had written the letter? How did they know that I'd be packing a bag to leave home? I couldn't figure any of these things out, let alone what the letter might mean!

But I didn't have time to think about all that now – the car taking me to Grandpa's was due any minute. What kind of tools do you need for an adventure? I had no idea, but I knew where to start looking…

I unlocked the steel door to Dad's laboratory and saw Rex snoozing on the floor. The fart gas must have been more powerful than I'd thought.

Tiptoeing into the room and holding my breath, I packed these things in my backpack:

- **Tranquillizer darts**
- **Dad's memory obliterator**
- **Camouflage paint**
- **Night-vision goggles**
- **Walkie-talkie earplugs**
- **A compass (that always points home)**
- **A bottle of truth serum**

- A stun gun
- A pen that can write in any language
- Super-strength fart gas (what was left of it)
- Morph's memory chips
- Steel rope
- Supersonic screecher

After my bag was full of Dad's inventions, I quietly walked past the T-rex. He looked so small and helpless, I had to take him with me and look after him.

And so I put the snoozing dinosaur and the bag of adventure tools next to the front door. Then I walked into the kitchen, opened the fridge and took out hot dogs, bacon, steaks and any other meat I could find. Rex would be really hungry when he woke up and I owed him a good meal after knocking him out with fart gas.

And then Grandpa's chauffeur, Stanley, was coming up the driveway. I've known Stanley for as long as I can remember. He does everything for Grandpa – he drives his cars, fixes Grandpa's garden fence when it's broken and does other things around the house too – things that my Grandpa is too old to do. Stanley is tall and thin and was born in England. He used to work for the President in the White House! How cool is that?

Anyway, Stanley drove me all the way to Grandpa's house in silence. Rex slept for the whole ride, but I couldn't. I didn't feel like reading a comic book, so I had lots of time to think about what had happened.

Maybe Mum and Dad were living in a cave with a pet Bugenasaura. Maybe they were cooking their food on a fire every night and drawing strange pictures on the wall. Maybe Dad was even trying to make another time machine out of leaves, dinosaur poop, tree bark and whatever else he could find in a prehistoric jungle.

One thing was for sure. As soon as I got to Grandpa Monty's, I had to find a way of fixing Morph and getting Mum and Dad back.

But there were other things that I needed to figure out too – like what that letter meant and exactly what kind of adventure I was going to have...

It was night time when I arrived at my new home. The private road leading to Grandpa's house is over a mile long, but finally we reached the front gates, and there in front of me was Solvit Hall.

Grandpa Monty's house is as big as a castle and pretty ancient. I got out of the car, slamming the door behind me. Stanley carried my bags and I carried my new pet T-rex.

"Henry!" Grandpa beamed at me as he swung open the solid oak front door.

"I'm Will, Grandpa," I said. "Henry's Dad's name."

"William, of course!" said Grandpa. "And who is this little sleepy rascal?" He pointed at Rex.

"This is Rex, Grandpa. The baby T-rex that I was telling you about."

Plato came bounding towards me, his fluffy white tail freezing in mid-wag as soon as he saw the sleeping dinosaur in my arms.

"I hope he'll be OK, Grandpa," I said, nodding down at Rex. I was a little worried that I'd hurt him with the fart gas – he'd been asleep for ages.

"There'll be a meat feast waiting for him when he wakes up, don't you worry!" Grandpa chuckled.

I followed Grandpa into the dark house, Plato whimpering behind us.

"Have you thought of a way to rescue Mum and Dad yet?" I yawned.

"All in good time," said Grandpa. "Let's talk about that in the morning. Best to get a good night's sleep first."

It was late and I was tired, so I decided that Grandpa was probably right about getting some sleep. He led me up the huge spiral staircase to my bedroom. It was lined with ancient family portraits with plaques under them, members of the Solvit family from centuries ago – mountaineers, naval commanders, deep-sea divers, explorers – all adventurers of some kind.

At the top of the stairs were pictures of my Grandpa and my dad. Their plaques just had their names and their birth dates. My dad's plaque said "Inventor," but my Grandpa's plaque didn't say anything at all. I knew my Grandpa had had a job when he was younger – Dad always told me that it was something very important. But I realized that I'd never been told what my Grandpa's job was... Right then, though, I was too tired to care. All I wanted to do was go to sleep.

Stanley put my bags on the bed and left Grandpa, Plato, Rex, and me alone in the room.

"We'll have fun together, Adam," said Grandpa, his pale eyes smiling as he spoke.

I was so tired, I didn't even bother to correct him.

"You just get some sleep, boy." Grandpa lifted Rex out of my hands, tucked him under his arm, and walked out without saying another word.

"Morning Henry," Grandpa said, as I plonked myself down in a chair.

"I'm Will, Grandpa," I reminded him.

"Juice?" he asked.

"Yes, please. Where's Rex?" I asked.

"In the greenhouse. I thought he'd feel at home among the tomato plants," replied Grandpa.

I shook my head and ran out of the kitchen, through the house and onto the lawn. As you can imagine, Grandpa's yard and gardens are huge. I sprinted over the grass, jumped over the vegetable patches and ran past the pond until I finally found the greenhouse.

At first I couldn't see anything, just loads of

WILL'S FACT FILE

Dear Adventurer,

As you know, dinosaurs roamed Earth for millions of years. They survived climate changes, continents shifting and the extinction of numerous other species. But something weird happened... the dinosaurs disappeared.

Check out my top dino facts over the next few pages and use the decoder to unlock the secret coded pictures.

Discovering Dinosaurs

From harmless herbivores like the Bugenasaura to fierce carnivores like the T-rex, there were many different species of dinosaurs that spanned millions of years of existence.

The Age of the Dinosaur is called the Mesozoic era and is divided into 3 time periods.

Triassic period – 251-200 million years ago
Jurassic period – 200-145 million years ago
Cretaceous period – 145-65 million years ago

DINO FACTS!

They were the most successful animals to ever live on the Earth.

DID YOU KNOW...

A person who studies dinosaurs is called a **palaeontologist!**

The Ornithopod dinosaurs had beaks like ducks!

Dinosaurs had scaly skin and laid eggs.

Meat-eating dinosaurs are called carnivores.

Dinosaurs mysteriously disappeared 65 million year ago.

Dinosaurs that ate only plants are called herbivores.

The theropods were the fastest dinosaurs. They were small, bird-like and walked on two legs.

The biggest dinosaur eggs were from the Hypselosaurus.

The Giganotosaurus was the biggest dinosaur ever to have lived.

COOL FACT: Over thousands of years, the bones, teeth and even poo of dead dinosaurs turned to rock called fossils.

Meat-eating dinosaurs relied on their speed and hunting skills for survival. They would eat anything that moved, including reptiles, mammals and even other dinosaurs!

Top 5 biggest meateaters

1. Spinosaurus 16 metres 9 tons
2. Giganotosaurus 15 metres 9 tons
3. Carchandontosaurus 13 metres 7 tons
4. Tyrannosaurus rex 12 metres 7.5 tons
5. Tarbosaurus 10 metres 4 tons

Even though the Giganotosaurus was huge, it could run up to 15mph.

Plant eaters were generally much bigger than their meat-eating cousins.

The mighty Brachiosaurus had unusually long front legs and at 6 metres in height was the tallest of all the dinosaurs.

Top 5 heaviest herbivores

1. Argentinasaurus 80 tons
2. Paralititan 64 tons
3. Sauroposeidon 60 tons
4. Brachiosaurus 40 tons
5. Seismosaurus 30 tons

Dinosaurs needed to be able to defend themselves. Some used their vast bulk and others had horns and plates to protect them. The Kentrosaurus was a prickly dinosaur with sharp spikes on its ail and hips. The Protoceratops lived in large herds or protection.

Guess the Dinosaurs...

Length: Up to 12 metres
Diet: Carnivorous
Period: Cretaceous
Adventurer Survival Fact:
These deadly predators have bad eyesight and can only see you if you move. Have you worked out the name of this dangerous dinosaur?

Answer: Tyrannosaurus Rex

Length: Up to 9 metres
Diet: Herbivorous
Period: Cretaceous
Adventurer Survival Fact: These dinosaurs won't eat you, but they could poke you to death! Have you guessed which dinosaur these clues are pointing to?

Answer: Triceratops

Length: Wingspan up to 10 metres
Diet: Carnivorous
Period: Late Triassic
Adventurer Survival Fact:
These creatures are dangerous as they swoop down from the skies and pluck their prey from the ground. Guessed the name of this dino yet?

swer: Pterodactyl

Length: Up to 5 metres
Diet: Herbivorous
Period: Jurassic
Adventurer Survival Fact:
These dinosaurs are covered in bony spikes or studs. Have you figured out the name of this dinosaur?

Answer: Stegosaurus

Length: Up to 10-20 metres.
Diet: Herbivorous
Period: Cretaceous
Adventurer Survival Fact:
These dinosaurs walked upright like birds. Have you worked out the name of this dinosaur?

Answer: Ornithopod

Length: 9 metres
Diet: Carnivorous
Period: Jurassic
Adventurer Survival Fact:
Its name means great lizard and it was probably a scavenger, eating flesh from an animal that was already dead.

Answer: Megalosaurus

Length: Around 10 metres
Diet: Herbivorous
Period: Late Jurassic
Adventurer Survival Fact:
It used its club tail to attack predators. The top of its body was covered with plates of bone. Can you guess the dinosaur?

Length: 25 metres
Diet: Herbivorous
Period: Late Jurassic
Adventurer Survival Fact:
It had a small head for its body and a tiny brain. Its front legs were longer than its back legs so its body sloped towards the tail. Have you guessed which dinosaur these clues are pointing to?

Length: 27 metres
Diet: Herbivorous
Period: Late Jurassic
Adventurer Survival Fact :
This dinosaur may have lived to be more than 100 years old. Place your decoder over this secret image.

Length: 15 metres
Diet: Carnivorous
Period: Cretaceous
Adventurer Survival Fact:
This dino was bigger than a T-rex and its teeth were an awesome 20 centimetres long. Have you worked out the name of this dangerous dinosaur?

Answer: Giganotosaurus

Length: 7 metres
Diet: Herbivorous
Period: Late Triassic
Adventurer Survival Fact:
This dinosaur had a long neck and a small head. Have you worked out the name of this dangerous dinosaur?

Answer: Plateosaurus

Length: Up to 17 feet
Diet: Carnivorous
Period: Early Jurassic
Adventurer Survival Fact: These dinosaurs were one of the biggest groups of sea reptiles. Do you know the name of this dinosaur?

Answer: Plesiosaurus

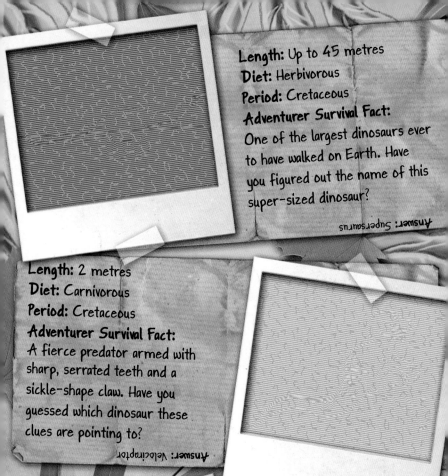

Length: Up to 45 metres
Diet: Herbivorous
Period: Cretaceous
Adventurer Survival Fact:
One of the largest dinosaurs ever to have walked on Earth. Have you figured out the name of this super-sized dinosaur?

Answer: Supersaurus

Length: 2 metres
Diet: Carnivorous
Period: Cretaceous
Adventurer Survival Fact:
A fierce predator armed with sharp, serrated teeth and a sickle-shape claw. Have you guessed which dinosaur these clues are pointing to?

Answer: Velociraptor

Length: 1 metre
Diet: Carnivorous
Period: Triassic
Adventurer Survival Fact:
One of the world's oldest dinosaurs, it moved around quickly on two long, slender legs. Do you know the name of this dinosaur?

Answer: Eoraptor

leafy tomato plants that looked like a small jungle. But then the leaves of the plants started rustling and Rex waddled towards me. He already looked bigger than he did when he'd hatched.

As I ran towards him, Rex dropped the raw steak he was chewing and looked happy to see me.

I carefully patted his bald, cold head. He purred and tried to nip me with his teeth.

"No, Rex. Bad T-rex! No biting!"

He blinked at me and then went back to his steak.

I watched him devour his meaty meal and dribble all over the floor. I wasn't sure how I'd ever be able to play with him – his teeth were as sharp as daggers. But, happy that Rex was OK, I went back inside.

It didn't take me long to settle in to Solvit Hall. But a whole week had passed since I'd been staying with Grandpa Monty and I still hadn't made any progress in rescuing my parents or getting any sort of sense out of Grandpa, for that matter.

I had always suspected that Grandpa Monty was nuts. Mum had scolded me for saying so, insisting that he was just 'eccentric'. But now I knew for sure that I was right and she had been wrong. Grandpa was as crazy as you could get. Crazier than crazy. If you looked the word 'crazy' up in a dictionary you'd see a picture of my

Grandpa Monty staring back at you! But not only was Grandpa Monty loony, it was obvious that he had a secret too and while I couldn't do anything about the time machine, I might as well find out what it was.

But how do you expose a secret? You can't just ask someone outright – they'd never tell you the truth. So for now I just tried my hardest to think of all the good things about my new home...

- Grandpa never told me when to go to bed or when to get up.
- He didn't care how much noise I made when I played computer games, cuz he couldn't hear all that well.
- He let me keep Rex as a pet – Dad would never have allowed that.

Aaaarrgghh...
He keeps eating my socks!

But there were not-so-good things too, and the absolute worst thing about my new home was that we lived too far away from my old school, so Grandpa was making me enrol in a new one...

Anyone who's ever started a new school knows how tough it can be. Everyone already has their friends and you have to try extra hard to talk to people.

I'd spent ages trying to convince Grandpa that trying to fix Morph was way more important than school, but he wasn't interested. Every time I tried to talk to him about rescuing Mum and Dad he just ignored me and started talking about something else.

And so, here I was now, at West Ridge.

But I couldn't tell anyone the truth about who I was or where I'd come from. No one would have understood my secret. The truth about Mum and Dad, Rex and Morph would only make life harder for me.

So I told lots of jokes instead. Like today:

Teacher: Open your textbooks to page thirty-seven.

Me: How many dinosaurs can fit in an empty box? One. After that, the box isn't empty any more! What does a Triceratops sit on? Its Tricerabottom! What do you call a fossil that doesn't ever want to work?

Zoe: Lazybones!

That's how I met Zoe. Like me, Zoe was once the new girl at school. She's been here a few months already. Apparently she used to live in Singapore, on the other side of the world, where

Lazy bones!

they have lizards the size of Labradors – cool or
what!

I slammed the front door behind me as hard as
I could. That way Grandpa would know I was
home. I'd had a bad day and didn't want to speak
to him. I saw the letter right away. It was sitting
on the hall table and had my name on it. It must
have come in the mail that day, but there was
no stamp or postmark. It was the same grown-up
handwriting as the other two envelopes. I picked
it up and studied it for clues as to who had sent it.

Grandpa must have picked it up after it fell
through the postbox. Maybe he knew who had
sent it?

I tried to think ahead and guess who could be

sending me these letters...

It couldn't be Grandpa – why would he write to me when we lived in the same house?

It couldn't be my mum or dad – they were stuck in a prehistoric jungle.

It couldn't be anyone from my old school trying to play a joke on me – they didn't know my new address.

It couldn't be anyone from my new school – they didn't know me when I got the first two letters.

I decided I'd go up to my room to open the letter. I began to walk towards the staircase and Plato came bounding towards me. He jumped up at me and barked with excitement.

I opened up the letter:

WHY ARE THERE OLD DINOSAUR BONES IN THE MUSEUM?

BECAUSE THEY CAN'T AFFORD NEW ONES!

IT'S BEEN A WHILE SINCE I LAST WROTE TO YOU, AND YOU STILL DON'T KNOW WHAT MONTY'S SECRET IS. IT'S NOT GOOD ENOUGH, WILL. YOU ARE NOT AN ORDINARY BOY AND YOU ARE NOT FROM AN ORDINARY FAMILY. YOU HAVE A VERY SPECIAL PURPOSE IN THIS WORLD. IT'S TIME TO GROW UP, WILL. YOU MUST FIND OUT WHAT MONTY'S SECRET IS. START WITH THE HOUSE. TAKE A LOOK AROUND, YOU NEVER KNOW WHAT YOU MIGHT FIND. EVERY PROBLEM HAS A SOLUTION. EVERY LOCK HAS A KEY. THESE LETTERS ARE YOUR SECRET TO KEEP. DON'T TELL ANYONE, NOT EVEN MONTY.

My face felt hot and my heart was beating fast. I was so confused about the letter – I didn't know what to do. I had all of these thoughts bouncing around my brain: What is Monty's secret? How am I supposed to find it out? What did the letter mean by 'a special purpose in this world'? Why did I need to look around my Grandpa's house? What was I going to find, and how would I know when I found it? Who was writing me these letters? And most important of all, how was any of this going to help me fix Morph and rescue Mum and Dad?

I sat in silence for ages. All I did was stare into space. Then Plato started to lick my hand – as if he was worried about me.

"Don't worry," I said. "Everything will be OK."

Then it suddenly became clear to me what I had to do. There was nothing else I could do. I had no choice – I had to do what the letter told me. Grandpa's house was a big house to explore, but tomorrow was Saturday – I'd have the whole weekend to find whatever I was looking for.

I leaped off the bed and onto my feet. Plato jumped on the floor and wagged his tail expectantly.

"Grandpa is hiding something from us, Plato," I said. "There's a secret in this house, and I intend to find it!"

The next day, after I'd done my morning dinosaur chores (Rex had moved into the yard – he'd grown way too big to be kept in the greenhouse), I ran back inside to start searching the house. I had no idea what I was supposed to be looking for. The letter had mentioned something about locks and keys, so I figured trying to open every door in the house would be a good place to start. I took a pen and notebook with me – I thought I'd make a list of anything interesting I found so I could look back over it later for any clues.

I decided that I'd start at the top of the house and work my way down. Plato followed me as I climbed the stairs to the attic, but the door was locked.

Since I couldn't get into the attic, I thought I'd start at the bottom of the house and work my way up instead. But there was really very little to note – other than a suitcase full of fake money. You see, I've watched enough detective shows to be able to tell when money's fake. Why would Grandpa Monty have a suitcase full of fake money? Maybe he's a con man? Maybe that's his secret? I slipped a bill into my pocket as evidence.

I spent ages going through the photo albums, looking for clues. I found a picture of Grandpa

in a soldier's uniform, lots of black-and-white photos of people I'd never seen before, and a picture of my dad when he was my age. I took the soldier picture just in case it was a clue to Grandpa's secret.

Grandpa was snoring loudly in an easy chair in the living room so I had to be quiet. There was nothing in there except chairs, lamps, paintings and rugs.

I lifted the paintings off the walls to see if there were secret safes behind them – nothing.

I looked underneath the rugs in case there were any secret trap doors – nothing.

Grandpa's study – I'm not supposed to go in there, so I had to be quick while Grandpa was sleeping. But there were just bookshelves with lots of books – including Beginner's Guide to Speaking Russian, Morse Code Dictionary, The Secret Lives

WHAT is
Grandpa's
secret?
?

? ?

of Birds and A-Z of Tanks – and a desk with lots of drawers.

I opened the desk drawers and found not one but three passports with Grandpa's photo in them! One was French and said his name was Philippe Zmirou, and one was German and said his name was Nicolai Weist! Definitely the most interesting find yet. I took all three passports as proof of some kind of shady secret.

Then I went into Mum and Dad's room – where they slept when we used to come and stay with Grandpa. But there were just some clothes, science magazines and a picture of me as a baby being held by Grandpa Monty.

I looked in all the other bedrooms (there are about fifteen), but there was nothing interesting to write about other than more dust, cobwebs, and a huge spider.

Then I went back to my room. I already knew what was in there, but I thought I'd check anyway.

Seeing Morph on my bedside table just reminded me of how I was no closer to being able to fix it. Whatever Grandpa's secret was, I hoped that it would help me travel back in time to rescue Mum and Dad.

I flicked through the dozens of programs on the memory chips that I could have used if Morph was working. Check out some of these cool programs:

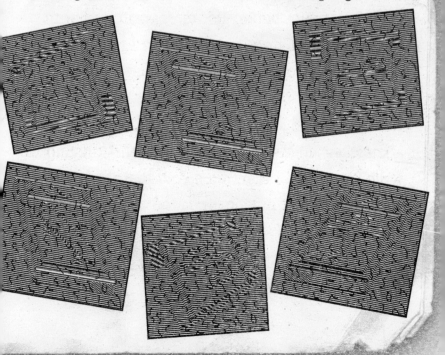

There were also a few programs that I wasn't too sure about – they had funny names like 'Arrival', '17' and 'Neptune'.

I put the memory chips down, sat on my bed and got out all of the things I'd collected from my search: the pictures, the fake money, the passports.

I still couldn't understand what the secret was – nothing seemed obvious to me. I shook my head, feeling really annoyed about everything, when the bookcase full of boring books opposite my bed caught my eye. I got up and walked towards it. Taking each book off the shelves one by one, I opened them and flicked through them – I wanted to check that there was nothing hiding inside.

I picked up the last book on the shelf: Romanian Folk Tales. The book was so old that the letters on the front had practically faded away. I opened the front cover and couldn't believe what I saw. The pages of the book had been cut out and in the middle was a key!

I got so excited I jumped up and down and Plato jumped up and down with me. He was barking like crazy and I had to quickly calm down to keep him quiet – I didn't want to wake Grandpa.

I ran out of the room and up the attic stairs. Plato started whimpering as we got closer.

I got to the door and slowly reached for the handle. As I took the key out of my pocket, I noticed that my hand was shaking. I put the key in the lock – it fit! Then I took a deep breath and turned the key. The lock clicked open and I pushed the door back.

Fumbling with my hand along the wall, I found a light switch. Dull orange light flooded the dusty

attic room. The room was packed with strange
and wonderful things – like an Aladdin's cave.
My mouth hung open, and I didn't even blink as I
looked around, trying to figure out what all of the
weird things were. In a way it was a lot like my
dad's laboratory – packed full of stuff that I had
no idea what to do with. One wall had a whole
load of swords mounted on it. The other walls
were lined with shelves crammed with all kinds
of crazy things. I tiptoed across the floor. Plato
whimpered and refused to come in.

I was walking towards the swords when I
tripped over a box in the middle of the floor.

It was made of dark wood and was covered
with dust, but I could see that it had a strange
symbol carved into the top of it. Weird!

I knelt on the grimy floor and started to run my
fingers over the surface, trying to find a way to

open it. I wanted to know what was inside! But no matter how hard I tried, the box wouldn't open.

I was trying so hard to get the box open that I almost didn't see the letter lying right next to it. It was exactly the same as all the others. The really strange thing was that, like everything else in the attic, the letter was covered with a layer of dust. I grabbed the envelope and ripped it open as quickly as I could.

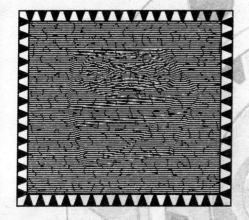

WHAT DO YOU CALL A DINOSAUR THAT NEVER GIVES UP?
TRY AND TRY AND TRY AND TRY-SERRATOPS!

IF YOU'RE READING THIS LETTER IN THE SPOT THAT I LEFT IT IN, THEN YOU'RE SITTING RIGHT NEXT TO THE BOX THAT WILL CHANGE YOUR LIFE FOREVER. YOU'RE NEARLY READY TO DISCOVER THE TRUTH, WILL. UNLOCK THIS BOX TO UNLOCK YOUR FUTURE. FOLLOW THE ANIMAL – THE ANIMAL IS THE KEY.

Obviously I had no idea what the letter meant. Plus, I was still no closer to finding out who was sending them all. But I was beyond excited! I was doing things right – I'd found the box – the clue that was going to help me find out the truth about

Grandpa once and for all.

'Follow the animal'. I thought for a second about what this might mean, and then I heard whimpering coming from behind me. Plato!

Follow the animal = follow Plato!

I stood up, picked up the box, and carried it with both hands. I walked towards the attic door and towards the fluffy white dog sitting just outside the room.

"Come on, then," I said to Plato, going back down the stairs to my room.

I hid the mysterious box underneath my bed and did as the letter told me, following Plato around.

In fact, I spent three whole hours following Plato wherever he went. Three hours in the shadow of a small, fluffy dog isn't that exciting!

It wasn't until he went upstairs to my room and

started chewing on the old, smelly sock I'd found lying under my bed that I started to think that maybe I'd gotten it wrong – Plato wasn't going to lead me anywhere interesting at all!

Then a thought struck me. . . Plato wasn't the only animal I could follow. There was another animal nearby that might lead me somewhere interesting, only this animal was a hundred times bigger and a million times more dangerous than Plato.

Rex!

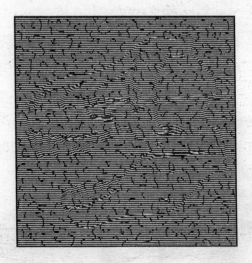

CHAPTER EIGHT
REX ON THE RUN

I headed for the backyard. Plato gave me a disappointed whimper as he followed me downstairs and watched me walk through the back door – he still wouldn't go anywhere near Rex.

Rex was fast asleep under the shade of a large tree in the corner of the yard. Apparently dinosaurs have to sleep a lot when they're growing. I was secretly pleased that Rex wasn't awake. Besides getting bigger, he was getting crankier by the day. Rex was now a teenage dinosaur – they're the worst: not yet full grown, but seriously moody!

zzzzzzzzzzzzzzzzzzzzzzzzzzzzz

Since Rex was busy sleeping, there was nowhere I could follow him. I decided to take a look around the yard, just in case there was anything important there that I was supposed to find.

As I was walking around, I saw the top of a dark-haired head quickly duck down behind a bush. Someone was there – spying on me! Someone who didn't want me to see them. I saw the swish of a brown ponytail at the side of the bush. I'd seen the same ponytail follow before – Zoe!

"Um… is he real?" she asked, pointing at Rex.

"What?" I asked.

"The dinosaur, is he real?" said Zoe.

I'd been busted!

"Uh… uh…" I stumbled around for the right words.

"I don't think it's safe to keep a pet T-rex, Will," said Zoe.

"Of course it's not safe!" I answered. "But I wasn't exactly given much choice."

I headed off back towards the house. I could feel Zoe following me, but I was too confused to turn around. How exactly was I going to be able to explain away a dinosaur?

Then I heard a strange growling – it was the sound of air being angrily huffed through dinosaur nostrils. I had thought Rex was asleep. I was wrong.

I heard the stomp of heavy dinosaur feet and the shrill sound of shrieking all at once. I turned around to see Rex heading straight for Zoe. His eyes were angry and his teeth were bared and he looked really, really annoyed.

"Rex, no!" I shouted.

But it was too late. He ran towards her, bent his head, and bit into her skirt. My heart stopped – I thought he was going to eat her in one bite!

Rex threw Zoe into the air and caught her with his tiny claws. He let out a loud roar and stomped towards the gate, which Zoe had left open. Before I could do anything, Rex was running across the lawn, over the hedge, through the vegetable patch, until he dipped out of sight. I could hear Zoe's frightened screams fade into the distance as he carried her away.

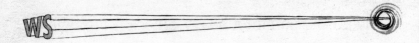

There wasn't a moment to waste.

I couldn't follow a T-rex unarmed and on foot – no way! I had to devise a plan. I ran into the house, skidding past Grandpa on my way.

"Hold on, Henry!" Grandpa called after me. "What is that blasted racket outside? I'm trying to sleep…"

"I'll explain later, Grandpa," I shouted behind me as I ran up the stairs. "And my name's Will!"

There was no time to stop and explain. If I didn't do something fast, Zoe would quickly become dino dinner!

I burst into my bedroom. I flung open the wardrobe doors and dug out the bag of stuff I'd taken from Dad's laboratory. I quickly picked out the things I'd need.

This is what I took:

- The electronic stun gun
- Dad's memory obliterator (if people were going to see a dinosaur running down the street, there was no way I could risk them remembering it and telling the world!)

She blinked at me and looked slightly confused.

"You be careful on that scooter, young man," she said. "You'll crush my flower beds!"

"It's not a scooter!" I shouted back at her. "It's a skateboard!"

I was just so relieved that the memory obliterator worked. I'd never used it before, but I'd seen Dad use it in emergencies. I figured that a T-rex on the loose was definitely an emergency, so I knew Dad would approve.

I did a sharp 180 degree turn as I zoomed around the corner onto Main Street. I couldn't believe the mess that lay ahead of me. As soon as I'd caught Rex and rescued Zoe I was going to be in so much trouble!

Store windows had been smashed by Rex's huge, swinging tail, and park benches flattened.

A tall man with red hair was trying to be brave

– he had grabbed a pole from a nearby hardware store and was headed in Rex's direction. I quickly blasted him with the memory obliterator.

Weaving my way through the crowd of frightened spectators, I headed towards the sound of thudding dinosaur steps.

The memory obliterator was on overdrive – I was blasting everyone I passed and sending a few extra blasts out into the crowd just in case I missed anyone. I was feeling pretty scared about what I was having to do and knew in my heart that I was going to have an even tougher job covering this up. The memory obliterator erased the last ten minutes of your memory and stopped you from forming new memories for the next few minutes, but would that be enough?

I was getting closer to Rex. I could see his heavy tail swinging around, knocking over

everything in sight. I could hear Zoe's screams.
She was alive!

"Wiiiiilllllll!" Zoe shrieked.

"It's OK!" I shouted. "I'm coming!"

Rex was in full view now, heading for an
alleyway ahead. I chased after him, blasting
everyone with the memory obliterator as I kick-
flipped my way down the street.

The alleyway was narrow, with wooden fences
at either side. Rex began to slow down. I had my
chance. I whipped out the stun gun and shot one
sharp shock into his scaly back. He jolted and let
out a massive roar of pain.

"Sorry," I apologized. "There's no other way."

Rex let go of Zoe. She landed on the hard
ground with a thud.

"Ouch!" she shouted. "Did you have to do that,
Will?"

"Next time I won't bother saving…"

"Rooooaaaaaaaaaarrrrrrrrr!" Rex interrupted me.

I zapped him in the back of the head with the stun gun once again, and he fell to the ground with a huge crash.

Hearing the sound of frantic footsteps behind me, I turned around to see a group of people running towards us in panic. They all spoke at once…

"What the…?"

"If I didn't know better I'd say that was a Tyrann—"

"It's not what it looks like," I reassured them as I held the memory obliterator towards the group.

"William Solvit!" said one of the ladies, recognizing me right away. "Your grandpa told me last year that you'd be coming to stay with him. He said you'd cause trouble, but he said nothing about this…"

Before I could let her finish I let out a huge blast of memory obliteration onto the crowd.

"Look!" I shouted, pointing to Main Street, away from Rex. I needed to create a distraction. "A tornado's hit town!"

I watched the small group jog away from me, towards the trashed street, and turned back to Zoe, who stared straight back at me.

We both lowered our eyes towards the unconscious T-rex sprawled on the ground.

For a moment, all I could hear was the sound of my thumping heartbeat. And then Zoe spoke.

"So what do we do now, Will?" she asked.

"I should never have let myself into your yard, Will," said Zoe, looking ashamed. "If I had known that you had a dangerous dinosaur as a pet I'd never have done it... But – where did you get him? And why didn't he just eat me? And what's that thing in your hand that you're shooting at people? Why can't they remember what they saw? Will?... Will?... Will? Say something, Will."

Zoe's words rushed over me in a blur. I didn't know what to say – I had no idea how to answer all her questions. I had so many questions myself.

"Did you hear what that woman said?" I asked her.

Zoe looked confused.

HOW did Grandpa know?

"She said that my Grandpa had told her last year that I was coming to live with him."

"What's so weird about that?"

"It's weird because Grandpa couldn't have known that then. It wasn't exactly... planned."

"Maybe she had it wrong," Zoe said.

"Maybe," I said. But I knew she didn't.

"Will," Zoe said, gently, "I think we should focus on the dinosaur. We can worry about the rest later."

"You're right," I agreed.

I held the memory obliterator towards Zoe and pressed the button. A look of horror crossed her face and she raised her hands, as if that would stop me.

But the memory obliterator didn't work. Nothing came out of it – there was no blue flash of energy.

"Will!" she said angrily.

This is TOO weird!

"Maybe the batteries are dead..." I muttered as I shook it back and forth.

"You can't do that to me," Zoe shouted. "We're in this together now."

"Oh, no, we're not. There's no way I can risk having you remember this," I answered.

"Well, I'm going to go home tonight and write all about this in my diary," said Zoe. "If you blast my memory after that, then I'll read all about what happened and remember it anyway."

I sighed. It looked like Zoe was right.

"Look, Will," she said, coming towards me, "I promise I won't say anything to anyone about this. You can trust me – I'm good at keeping secrets."

"Zoe..."

She cut me off – I couldn't get a word in edgewise.

"I won't tell anyone about this – ever," she

went on. "You have my word."

I didn't know what to say.

"I'll help you with your maths homework..." she offered.

That was it. She'd won me over! "OK, I'll think about it," I said.

"Thanks, Will!" She smiled. "So what are we going to do about... you know..."

"About Rex? I'll stay here with him, in case he wakes up," I said. "Can you run back to my house as quickly as you can and tell my Grandpa what's happened?"

"Sure," she said.

I sank to my knees and knelt next to Rex.

"I'm sorry," I whispered to him. "I should never have taken..."

I didn't finish what I was saying, though. I was too busy staring at what was in front of me.

Wedged into the wooden alleyway fence was an envelope. Hastily I took the letter out and read:

WHAT DO YOU CALL A DINOSAUR THAT SMASHES EVERYTHING IN ITS PATH?
TYRANNOSAURUS WRECKS!

IT WAS WORTH THE CHASE. HERE IS THE KEY THAT YOU NEED.

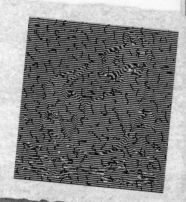

A small disk with a symbol on it hung on a long leather cord. It looked more like an amulet than a key. The symbol was exactly the same as the one on the box I had found in the attic.

I was looking at the amulet when I realized something: the person writing the letters must have known that Rex was going to run down the alleyway, and they must have known that this was where I'd knock him unconscious with the stun gun. Why else would they tell me to follow him? Why else would they leave an envelope with the key to the box in this exact spot?

But how could someone know which direction Rex would run? Unless... unless it was someone from the future looking back at every move I made.

One thing I did know for sure – if I was right and whoever was writing to me was from the future, then time travel was definitely involved. They'd have had to travel back in time to plant the letters for me to read. And if time travel was involved, then so was a time machine.

If I found the person writing to me, then I'd also find their time machine – then I'd have a way to rescue my parents and take Rex back to his rightful home.

I slipped the amulet around my neck for safekeeping and tucked it into my T-shirt so no one could see it.

I heard the patter of footsteps coming towards me.

I looked up, thinking it might be Zoe on her way back from Grandpa's, but it wasn't.

Two grown men, dressed head to toe in dark clothes, came over. And now I could hear the roar of a helicopter looming above, lowering ropes to harness around Rex and lift him into the air.

"We've come for the T-rex," said one of the men. "We were sent by Montgomery Solvit — we're old friends of his."

"My Grandpa sent you?" I asked. "Where will you take Rex?"

"Back to Solvit Hall immediately. Monty is

currently speaking to our employers to arrange a more… permanent location for the beast."

"The beast?" I looked shocked. I'd grown pretty fond of Rex, you see, so I didn't like hearing him talked about like that. "You're taking him there by helicopter?" I asked. "But people will see him in the sky…"

"We have ways of making them forget," said the man.

"I guess Grandpa won't let me keep him after what happened today," I said.

"No. Excuse us… we need to winch the beast up."

"His name is Rex," I said quietly.

They threw a sack over Rex and harnessed him in. Then the helicopter winched him up with the two men before flying away. Watching, I felt a lump in my throat as Rex was taken away from me and the dinosaur-shaped sack disappeared into the distance. I felt bad about zapping him. But maybe this was the right thing to do. It wasn't fair to keep him any longer.

I didn't want to go home and face up to what had happened. I couldn't face seeing Grandpa.

But then I remembered the amulet and the box that it was going to open. I wanted to know what was in that box more than anything.

I picked up my skateboard and started for home.

Totally cool board for busting out tricks

As I skated down the road leading to the house, I thought about the possible punishments that Grandpa was likely to dish out. OK, so he might send me to military school, but it wasn't as if I had any friends who would miss me, and Mum and Dad would come and rescue me as soon as they got back – if they ever got back. He could forbid me to have pets ever again, but to be honest, as much as I loved Rex, I'd had enough pet problems to last me a lifetime. He could make me give up my computer games – that would be the worst punishment EVER!

I opened the front door of Solvit Hall and took

a deep breath. The house was cold, dark and quiet. I rested my skateboard against the wall and stepped into the hallway. As my eyes adjusted to the darkness, all I could hear was the ticking of the grandfather clock and the whistle of a kettle coming from the kitchen.

Plato trotted into the hallway and wagged his tail when he saw me.

"Hey," I whispered, as I walked towards him.

Plato led me into the kitchen, where Grandpa was stirring a steaming cup of tea and flicking through the pages of a newspaper.

"Sit down, Will," he said, without even looking at me. It was the first time he'd ever said my name right – a sure sign that I was in big trouble. I slumped into one of the kitchen chairs and stared into my lap as I twiddled my thumbs, bracing myself for whatever harsh punishment was coming my way.

"I spoke to your friend," said Grandpa. "What was her name?"

"Zoe," I told him.

"Zoe! Yes, lovely girl. She told me everything. I told her to go home and rest up. She might come over for dinner tomorrow."

"Grandpa, I'm sorry," I blurted out. My face burned bright red as I looked over at him. He didn't once look up from his paper to meet my eyes. "I should never have tried to keep a pet dinosaur, I was being stu—"

"What happened today was not your fault," Grandpa said, now looking me right in the eye. He didn't seem like a crazy person as he spoke to me – he seemed to know exactly what he was talking about.

"It was not the fault of your friend or Rex. He's

a wild animal. A very dangerous, powerful, and unpredictable creature. I should have sent Rex away as soon as he hatched, but I could see how attached you were to him already, having lost your parents and everything."

"So I'm not in trouble?" I was amazed.

"No. Quite the contrary – you proved yourself to be quick-thinking, resourceful and brave," said Grandpa. "I was very proud of you today."

"So what will happen to Rex?" I asked, my voice trembling as I spoke. I couldn't decide if I was angry or upset.

"I know a man…" Grandpa looked down at his paper once again. He flicked through the pages as he spoke, as if what he was saying wasn't important at all. "… a very old, very dear friend of mine, who has his own island. The island is in the middle of the ocean and no one but he ever goes there. I have arranged for Rex to be flown out first thing tomorrow. He'll live there until we can find a way to send him back in time to where he's supposed to be."

"Are there other dinosaurs on the island?" I asked.

Grandpa looked at me with a knowing glint in his eye. "There are many special things on the island," he said, smiling. "I can promise you that it's the only place in the world that Rex will be safe and happy. Maybe one day I'll take you to visit him."

I wanted to thank Grandpa Monty for helping me, but I didn't know what to say. I wanted to ask him about the letters, about the amulet that I'd found, about the box in the attic and the secret that I knew he was keeping.

But there was no point in saying anything until

I had all the evidence I could find. I had to open that box. I had to know what was inside.

"I'm just going to my bedroom for a while," I muttered under my breath as I left the kitchen. I thought I saw Grandpa smile to himself, but I was gone too quickly to be sure.

I took the stairs two at a time and headed straight for my bedroom. I heard Plato yap at the sound of my hurried footsteps. "Not now," I said gently. "I need to be alone."

As soon as I was inside my room I dived under my bed and pulled out the box that I'd found in the attic.

This was it – the moment I'd been waiting for. I'd followed every clue and done everything the letters had told me to do. Was I finally going to be able to unlock the truth?

5th November 1955

I'm settling in to my new assignment. I've been at sea for three days now, and we're two days away from Russian waters.

Another letter came today. Just as before, there was no return address and no clue as to who sent it. How did the letter find me out here on the open ocean?

The letter's instructions were clear: Go to Moscow, spy on the army general and uncover his plans for the invasion of Europe. It's been 15 years since the first letter arrived; 15 years since I discovered what my destiny was. All this time I've been having adventures and learning how to become the best spy I can possibly be.

I sometimes wonder what it would be like to have been born into another family. I'm sure my life would have been easier if I wasn't an Adventurer. But I am a Solvit, and the latest in a long line of Adventurers.

Every child born into the Solvit family will become an Adventurer, whether they like it or not. Each of us must discover our special set of skills that will help us deal with our adventures.

My father was an explorer, my grandfather was a linguist. I am a spy. I wonder what my children and grandchildren will be...

I must go. I'll write again tomorrow.

Monty

It all made sense. The fake passports, the cases of fake money – I couldn't believe it! How exciting... how amazing... how totally awesome! Grandpa Monty, the old man who forgot my name and read about golf all day long, used to be a spy. That was his secret!

I quickly flicked through the rest of the diary. It

was full of spy tips and stories, but before I read the rest of it, I had to speak to Grandpa. The time had finally come to confront him about everything I knew. I needed to know what an "Adventurer" was. Was I one too? Was my dad one? Was that why he was stuck back in time? The diary said that Grandpa had received letters too. My letters must be from the same person – Grandpa Monty could tell me who it was!

CHAPTER ELEVEN
SECRETS UNCOVERED

I ran downstairs with the diary in my hand. Grandpa hadn't moved from the kitchen. He was still sitting and reading the paper with Plato sprawled at his feet.

He didn't look up as I started talking.

"Grandpa, I know," I said. I was speaking at a hundred miles an hour. "I know that you were a spy. I found your diary hidden in a box in the attic."

Grandpa didn't say anything. He pretended that he hadn't heard me. I walked around and stood right next to him.

"Grandpa, I've been getting letters – like the

ones that you got when you were younger. Why is everyone in the Solvit family an Adventurer? How do I become one? What did you mean in your diary when you said that we all have to find our 'special set of skills'? How can I find out what I'm supposed to be?"

Grandpa still didn't say anything. He didn't even look up.

"Grandpa!" I shouted.

"Glass of juice?"

"Grandpa, didn't you hear me?" I asked in disbelief. "I know your secret. I know that you were a spy. And I need to become an Adventurer. But I don't know how to become one or what I'm supposed to do. I need you to help!"

"What you need, Will," Grandpa said, "is to calm down and have a glass of juice."

I sat down, too stunned to speak. Grandpa

wasn't denying anything. It was all true.

"I need a biscuit," I finally said as Grandpa put his glass of juice down.

"Biscuits aren't really good for you, you know," Grandpa said, frowning. "If you want some, then you'll have to get them yourself. The biscuit jar's in the cupboard."

I opened the cupboard and picked up the biscuit jar. Beneath it was an envelope with my name on it. I turned around and looked at Grandpa in astonishment.

"Are you writing the letters, Grandpa?" I asked.

"If I'm writing the letters, then who wrote the letters to me?"

"I don't know."

"No, Will. I'm not the author of your letters. And I can't tell you who is writing them."

I ripped open the letter and read it quickly.

WHICH DINOSAUR SLEPT ALL DAY?
THE DINO-SNORE!

CONGRATULATIONS.
YOU HAVE PROVED YOURSELF TO HAVE WHAT IT
TAKES TO FULFIL YOUR DESTINY AND BECOME AN
ADVENTURER.
WELCOME TO A BRAVE NEW WORLD, WILL.
NOW YOU KNOW THE TRUTH ABOUT YOUR FAMILY
AND THE PERSON YOU MUST GROW UP TO BE. JUST
LIKE EVERY MEMBER OF THE SOLVIT FAMILY, YOU
ARE TO BE AN ADVENTURER.
EVERY SOLVIT ADVENTURER HAS HIS OR HER
OWN SPECIAL SKILL. YOUR DAD IS AN INVENTOR
AND YOUR GRANDPA IS A SPY. NOW YOU MUST FIND
YOURS. HAVE FAITH IN THE FUTURE AND DON'T
WORRY ABOUT THE PAST. DO NOT TRY TO FIND YOUR
PARENTS, WILL. THEY WILL FIND YOU WHEN THE
TIME IS RIGHT.
ONE LAST THING — IT'S TIME TO FIX MORPH. YOU
HAVE A DISK TO REBOOT HIM. IT'S MADE OF GAS. IT
HAS A RING AROUND IT, AND IT IS THE 8TH PLANET
FROM THE SUN.

"Grandpa! The letter tells me how to fix Morph! I can go back in time and rescue Mum and Dad!"

"And what else does it say?"

I read the letter, word for word, to Grandpa.

"Ah, riddles, fiddles. Fun, fun, fun!" Grandpa said with a smile. "But remember," he added seriously, "the letter warns you not to go searching for your parents. As you now know, your father is an Adventurer. He has important things to do – I imagine he's doing them right now. Besides, I think you've had enough adventure for one day. Why don't you drink your juice and leave time travel until tomorrow."

I thought about the riddle in the letter... What was the eighth planet from the sun? It was a planet that was made of gas and had a ring around it...

I ran upstairs and into my room. I opened my bedside table drawer, rummaged around and pulled out one of the memory chips.

I found the program I was looking for.

Neptune.

I slotted the chip into the drive. Success! A light flickered on and Morph's motor started to whirr into action.

I'd done it – Morph had rebooted!

But my heart sank when I remembered that the time machine chip had been crushed the last time I'd used Morph. Without that I had no way to travel back in time.

I had a quick look inside the drawer, but couldn't find a spare time travel memory chip. The first thing I'd do when I got Mum and Dad back, I decided, was make Dad start backing up all of his programs!

But even without a time machine, I still had Morph. I had the only existing device that could become whatever I wanted it to be. I could turn it into a plane and fly all the way around the world until I found another inventor who could make me a time machine program. I could turn Morph into a submarine and swim through the oceans of the earth until I found the island that they were taking Rex to. I could even turn it into a roller-coaster— that wouldn't help me save Mum and Dad, but it would be seriously fun! Whatever Morph became and wherever I went, there was one thing I knew for sure. I would find my mum and dad.

Rescuing them was going to be my first Adventure, or my second if you counted this one! Maybe Dad could help me discover what my adventuring skill was going to be – he always had an answer for everything.

The letter was right. I was in a brave new world now, a world where I was an Adventurer with a machine that could be anything and a diary that told me every spy trick I would ever need.

A smile crept over my face.

I couldn't wait...

Several hundred cats were gathered in a clearing, howling excitedly under the lights of the strange aircraft.

As we arrived, the lights vanished and the aircraft zoomed off. The cats arched their backs and circled us, hissing angrily.

They were going to attack us!

The adventure continues...

OTHER BOOKS IN THE SERIES